Plants vs. Zombies

BOOM BOOM MUSHROOM #1

ABDO
Spotlight

DARK HORSE BOOKS

PopCap

Written by **PAUL TOBIN**

Art by **JACOB CHABOT**

Colors by **MATT J. RAINWATER**

Letters by **STEVE DUTRO**

Cover by **JACOB CHABOT**

President and Publisher **MIKE RICHARDSON**
Editor **PHILIP R. SIMON**
Assistant Editor **MEGAN WALKER**
Designer **BRENNAN THOME**
Digital Art Technician **CHRISTINA McKENZIE**

Special thanks to Leigh Beach, Gary Clay, A.J. Rathbun, Kristen Star, Jeremy Vanhoozer, and everyone at PopCap Games. Editorial thanks to Sal Paradise.

DarkHorse.com | PopCap.com

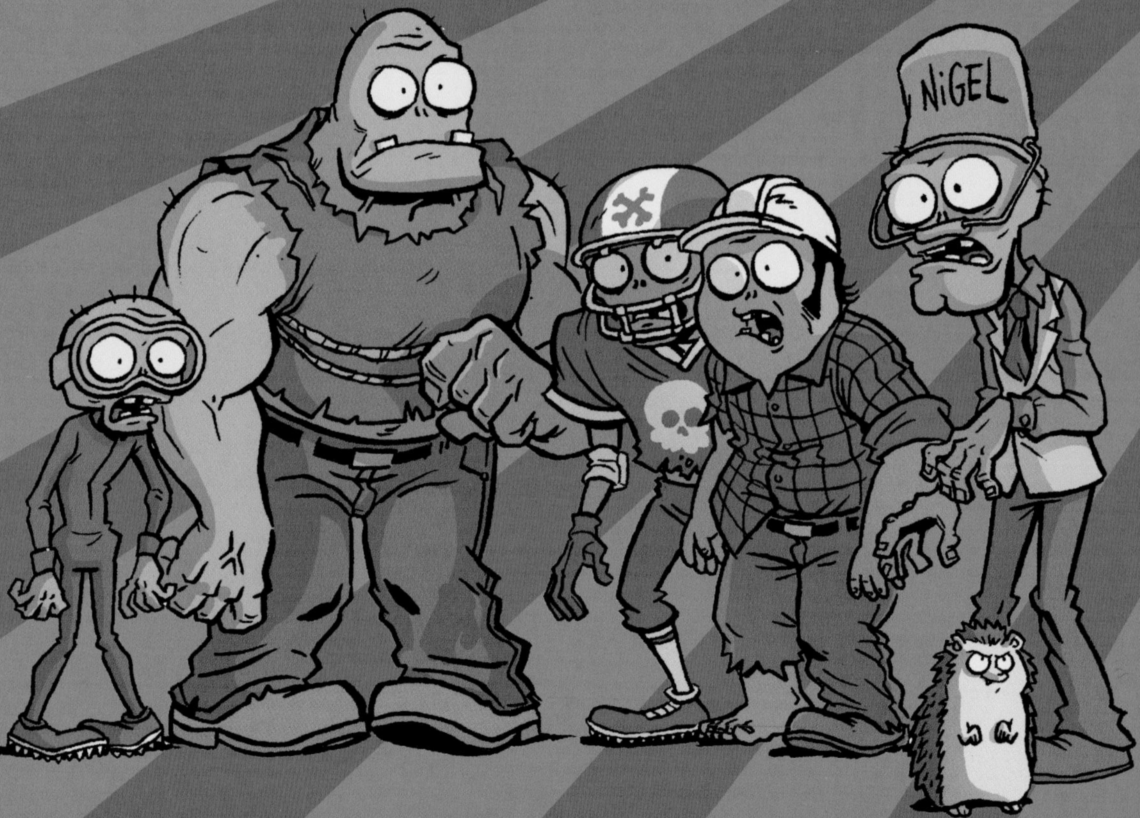
NiGEL

PLANTS VS. ZOMBIES™

BOOM BOOM MUSHROOM #1

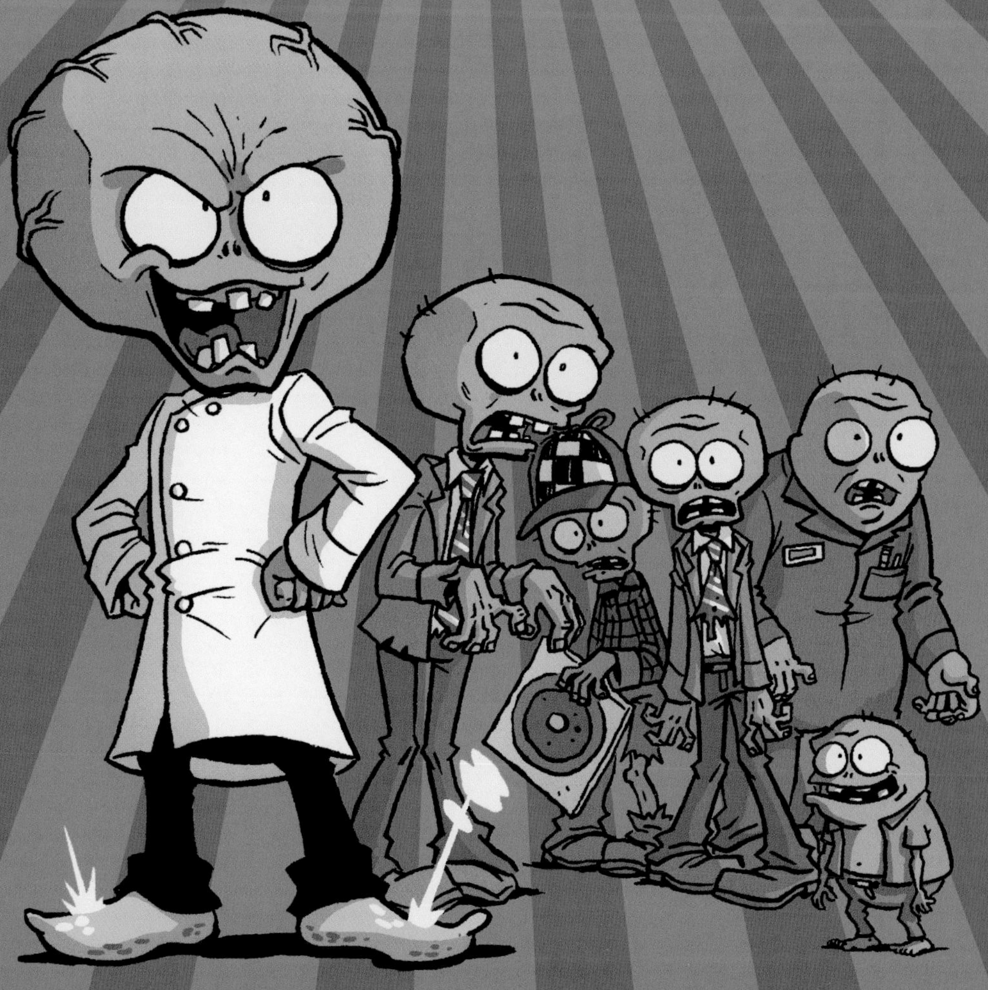

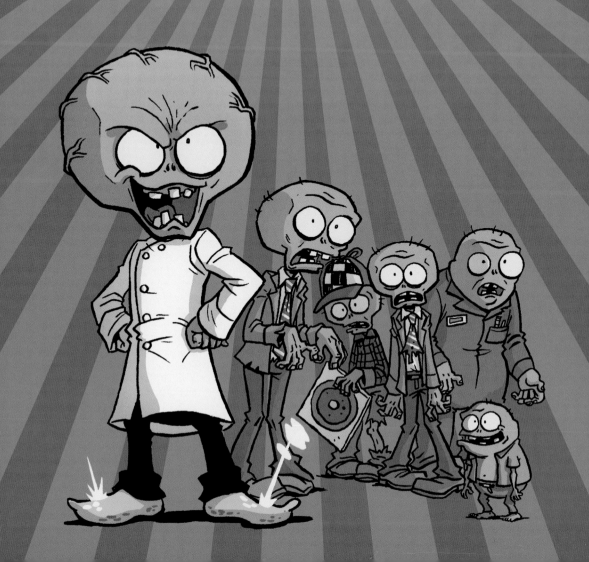

ABDOPUBLISHING.COM

Reinforced library bound edition published in 2018 by Spotlight, a division of ABDO, PO Box 398166, Minneapolis, Minnesota 55439. Spotlight produces high-quality reinforced library bound editions for schools and libraries.
Published by agreement with Dark Horse Comics.

Printed in the United States of America, North Mankato, Minnesota.
092017
012018

THIS BOOK CONTAINS
RECYCLED MATERIALS

DARK HORSE BOOKS

PopCap

Originally issued as Plants vs. Zombies #10: Boom Boom Mushroom Part 1 by Dark Horse Comics in 2016.

PUBLISHER'S CATALOGING IN PUBLICATION DATA

Names: Tobin, Paul, author. | Chabot, Jacob ; Rainwater, Matthew J., illustrators.
Title: Boom Boom Mushroom / by Paul Tobin ; illustrated by Jacob Chabot and Matthew J. Rainwater.
Description: Minneapolis, MN : Spotlight, 2018 | Series: Plants vs. Zombies
Summary: When Patrice and Nate discover Zomboss's plan to raise an underground zombie army, they must race to find the rare Boom Boom Mushroom before Zomboss puts his plan in motion.
Identifiers: LCCN 2017941916 | ISBN 9781532141249 (v.1 : lib. bdg.) | ISBN 9781532141256 (v.2 : lib. bdg.) | ISBN 9781532141263 (v.3 : lib. bdg.)
Subjects: LCSH: Plants--Juvenile fiction. | Zombies--Juvenile fiction. | Adventure and adventurers--Juvenile fiction. | Comic books, strips, etc.--Juvenile fiction. | Graphic novels--Juvenile fiction.
Classification: DDC 741.5--dc23
LC record available at http://lccn.loc.gov/2017941916

Spotlight

A Division of ABDO
abdopublishing.com

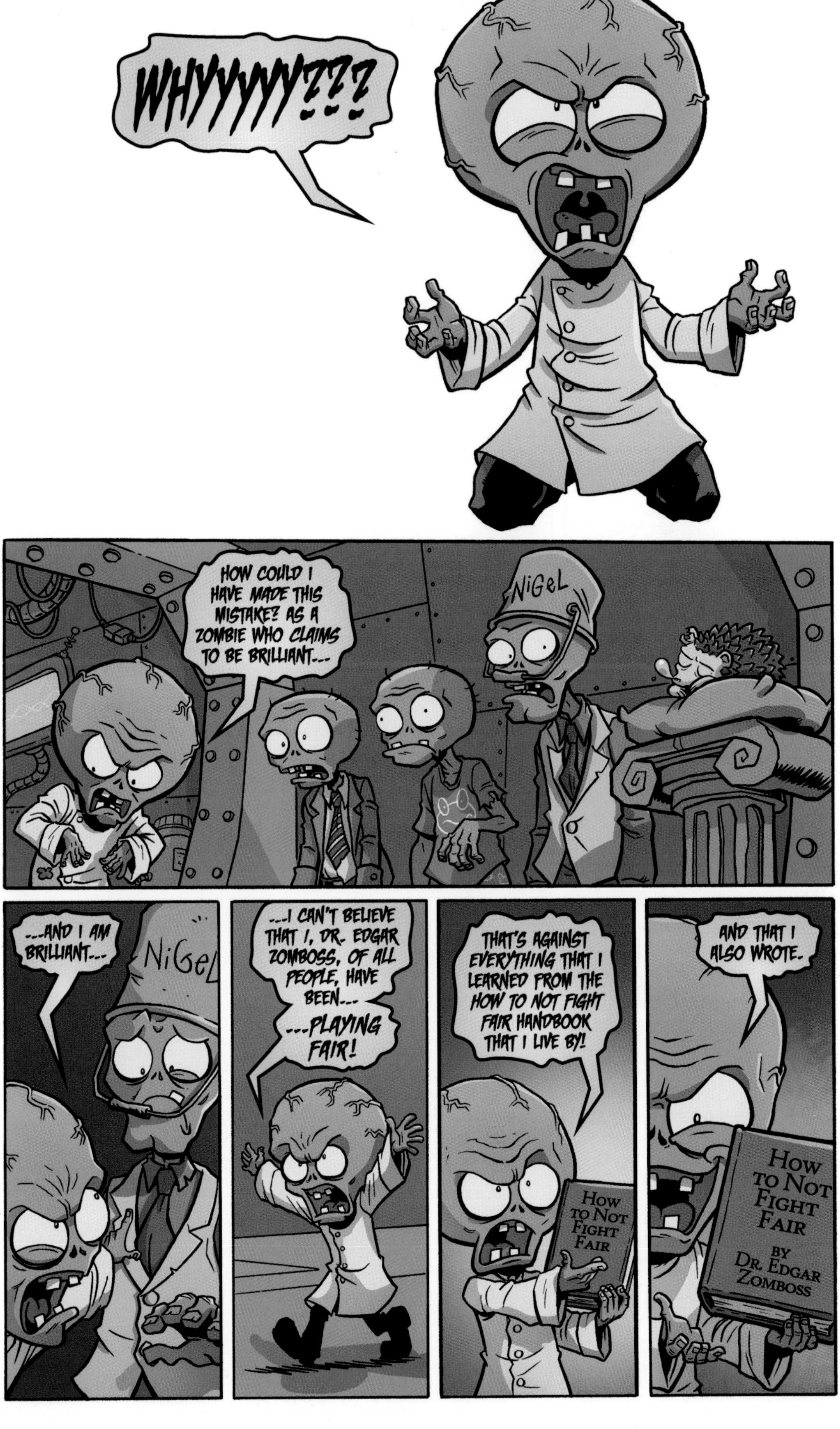
WHYYYYY???
HOW COULD I HAVE MADE THIS MISTAKE? AS A ZOMBIE WHO CLAIMS TO BE BRILLIANT...
NiGeL
...AND I AM BRILLIANT...
NiGeL
...I CAN'T BELIEVE THAT I, DR. EDGAR ZOMBOSS, OF ALL PEOPLE, HAVE BEEN...
...PLAYING FAIR!
THAT'S AGAINST EVERYTHING THAT I LEARNED FROM THE HOW TO NOT FIGHT FAIR HANDBOOK THAT I LIVE BY!
How to Not Fight Fair
AND THAT I ALSO WROTE.
How to Not Fight Fair
by Dr. Edgar Zomboss

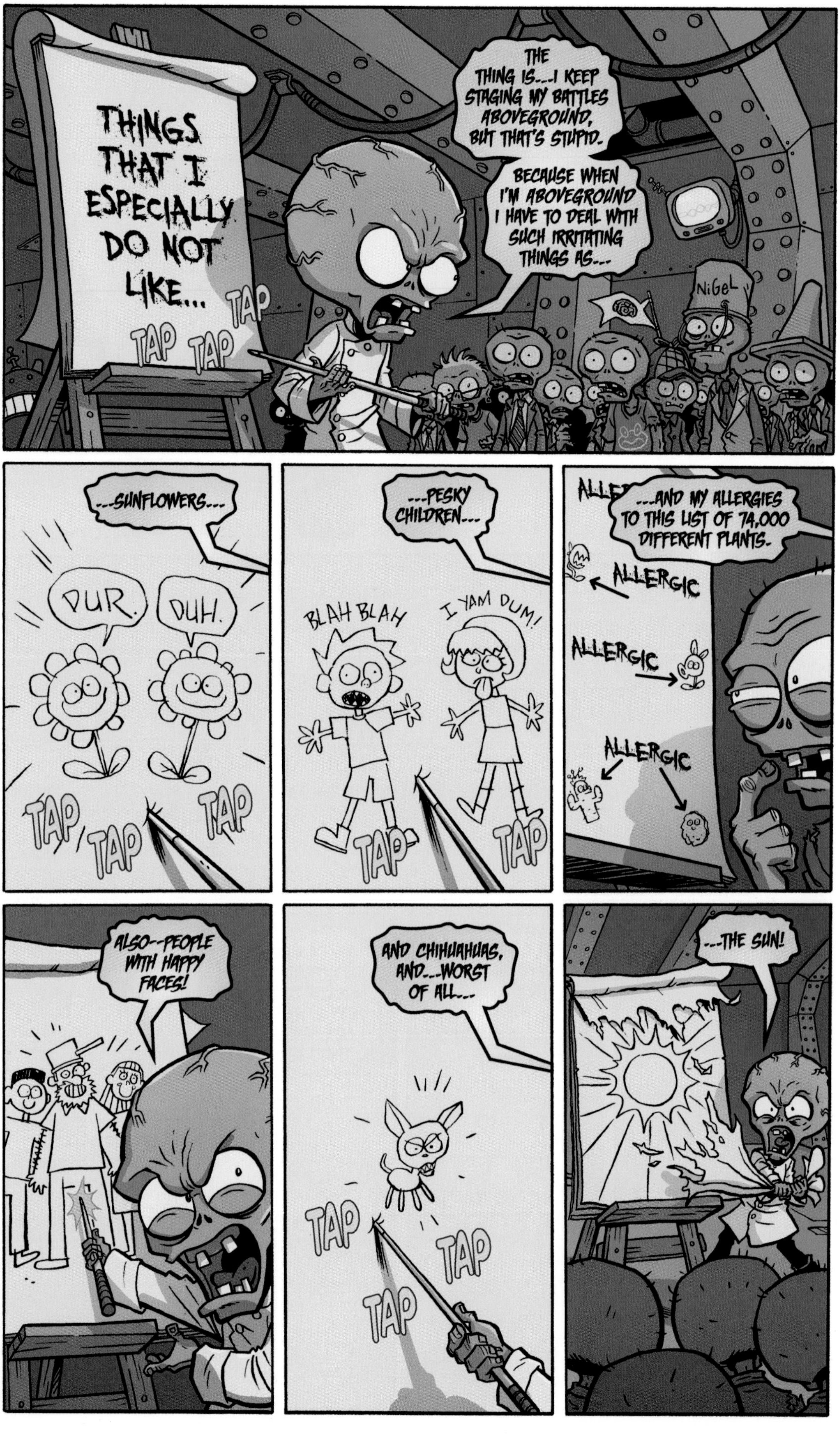
THINGS THAT I ESPECIALLY DO NOT LIKE...
THE THING IS...I KEEP STAGING MY BATTLES ABOVEGROUND, BUT THAT'S STUPID.
BECAUSE WHEN I'M ABOVEGROUND I HAVE TO DEAL WITH SUCH IRRITATING THINGS AS...
TAP TAP TAP
NiGeL
...SUNFLOWERS...
DUR.
DUH.
TAP TAP TAP
...PESKY CHILDREN...
BLAH BLAH
I YAM DUM!
TAP TAP
...AND MY ALLERGIES TO THIS LIST OF 74,000 DIFFERENT PLANTS.
ALLERGIC
ALLERGIC
ALLERGIC
ALSO--PEOPLE WITH HAPPY FACES!
AND CHIHUAHUAS, AND...WORST OF ALL...
TAP TAP TAP
...THE SUN!

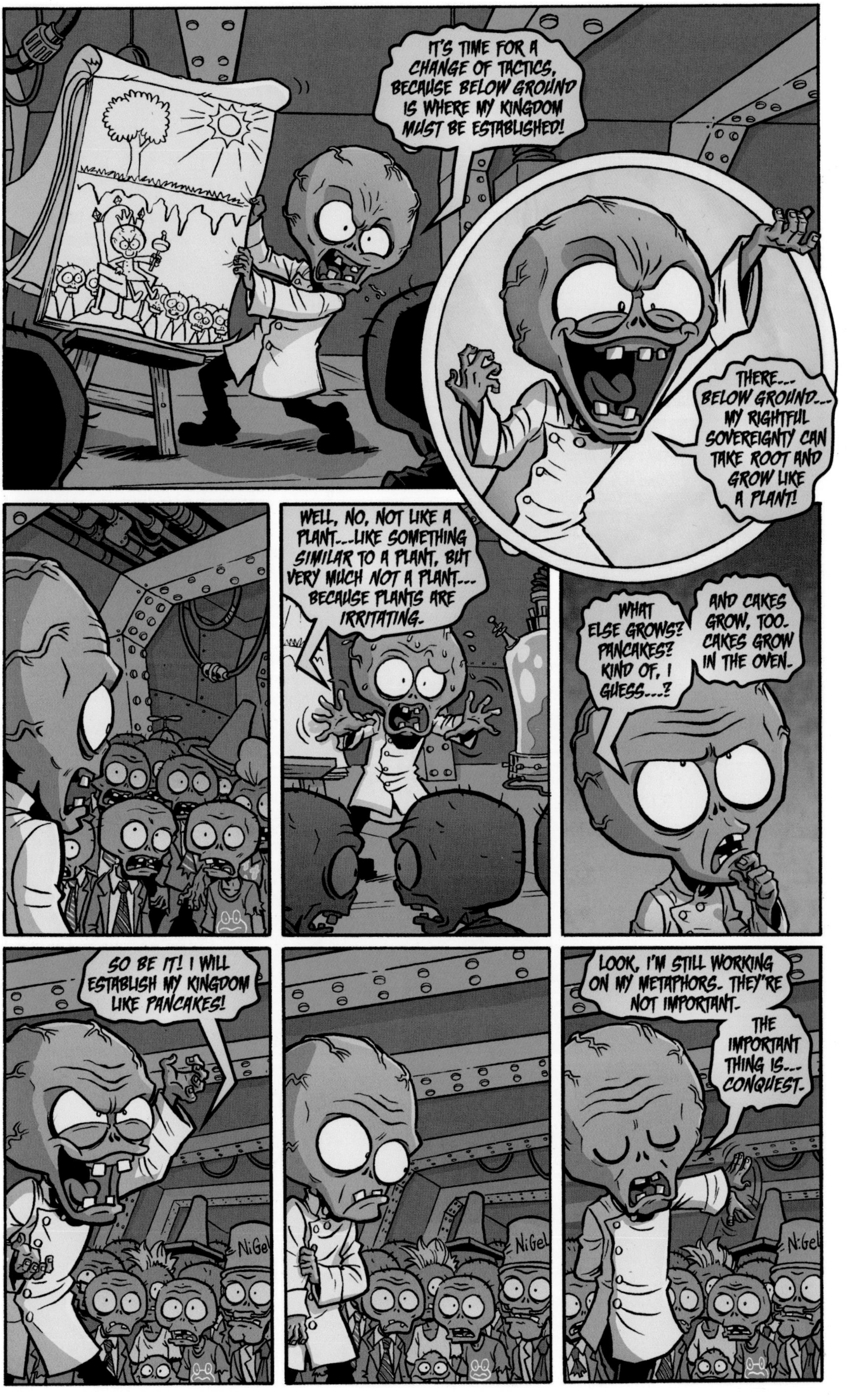
IT'S TIME FOR A CHANGE OF TACTICS, BECAUSE BELOW GROUND IS WHERE MY KINGDOM MUST BE ESTABLISHED!
THERE... BELOW GROUND... MY RIGHTFUL SOVEREIGNTY CAN TAKE ROOT AND GROW LIKE A PLANT!
WELL, NO, NOT LIKE A PLANT...LIKE SOMETHING SIMILAR TO A PLANT, BUT VERY MUCH NOT A PLANT... BECAUSE PLANTS ARE IRRITATING.
WHAT ELSE GROWS? PANCAKES? KIND OF, I GUESS...?
AND CAKES GROW, TOO. CAKES GROW IN THE OVEN.
SO BE IT! I WILL ESTABLISH MY KINGDOM LIKE PANCAKES!
NiGel
NiGel
LOOK, I'M STILL WORKING ON MY METAPHORS. THEY'RE NOT IMPORTANT.
THE IMPORTANT THING IS... CONQUEST.
NiGel

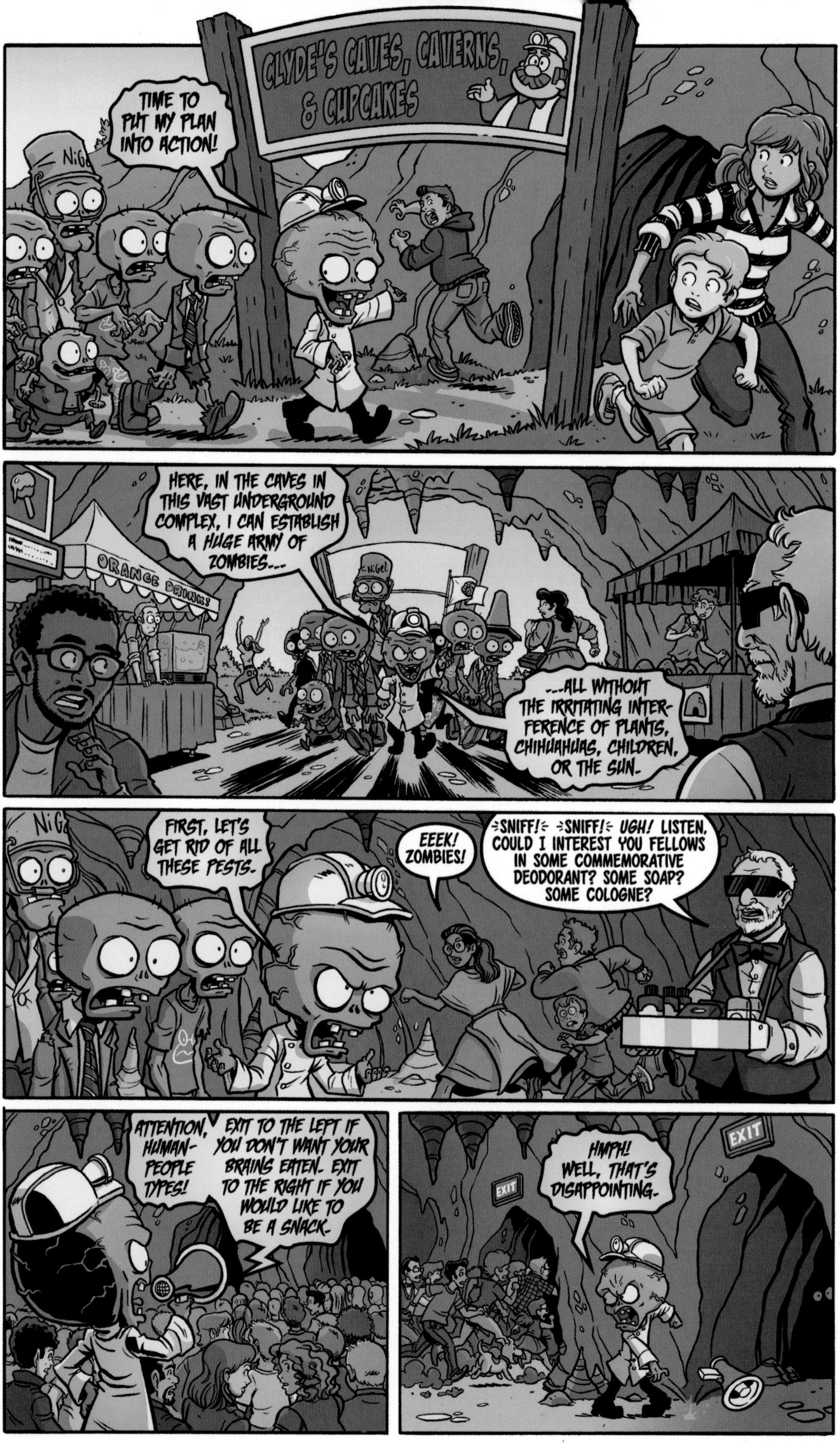
CLYDE'S CAVES, CAVERNS, & CUPCAKES
TIME TO PUT MY PLAN INTO ACTION!
HERE, IN THE CAVES IN THIS VAST UNDERGROUND COMPLEX, I CAN ESTABLISH A HUGE ARMY OF ZOMBIES...
ORANGE DRINKS
...ALL WITHOUT THE IRRITATING INTERFERENCE OF PLANTS, CHIHUAHUAS, CHILDREN, OR THE SUN.
FIRST, LET'S GET RID OF ALL THESE PESTS.
EEEK! ZOMBIES!
=SNIFF!= =SNIFF!= UGH! LISTEN, COULD I INTEREST YOU FELLOWS IN SOME COMMEMORATIVE DEODORANT? SOME SOAP? SOME COLOGNE?
ATTENTION, HUMAN-PEOPLE TYPES!
EXIT TO THE LEFT IF YOU DON'T WANT YOUR BRAINS EATEN. EXIT TO THE RIGHT IF YOU WOULD LIKE TO BE A SNACK.
EXIT
EXIT
HMPH! WELL, THAT'S DISAPPOINTING.

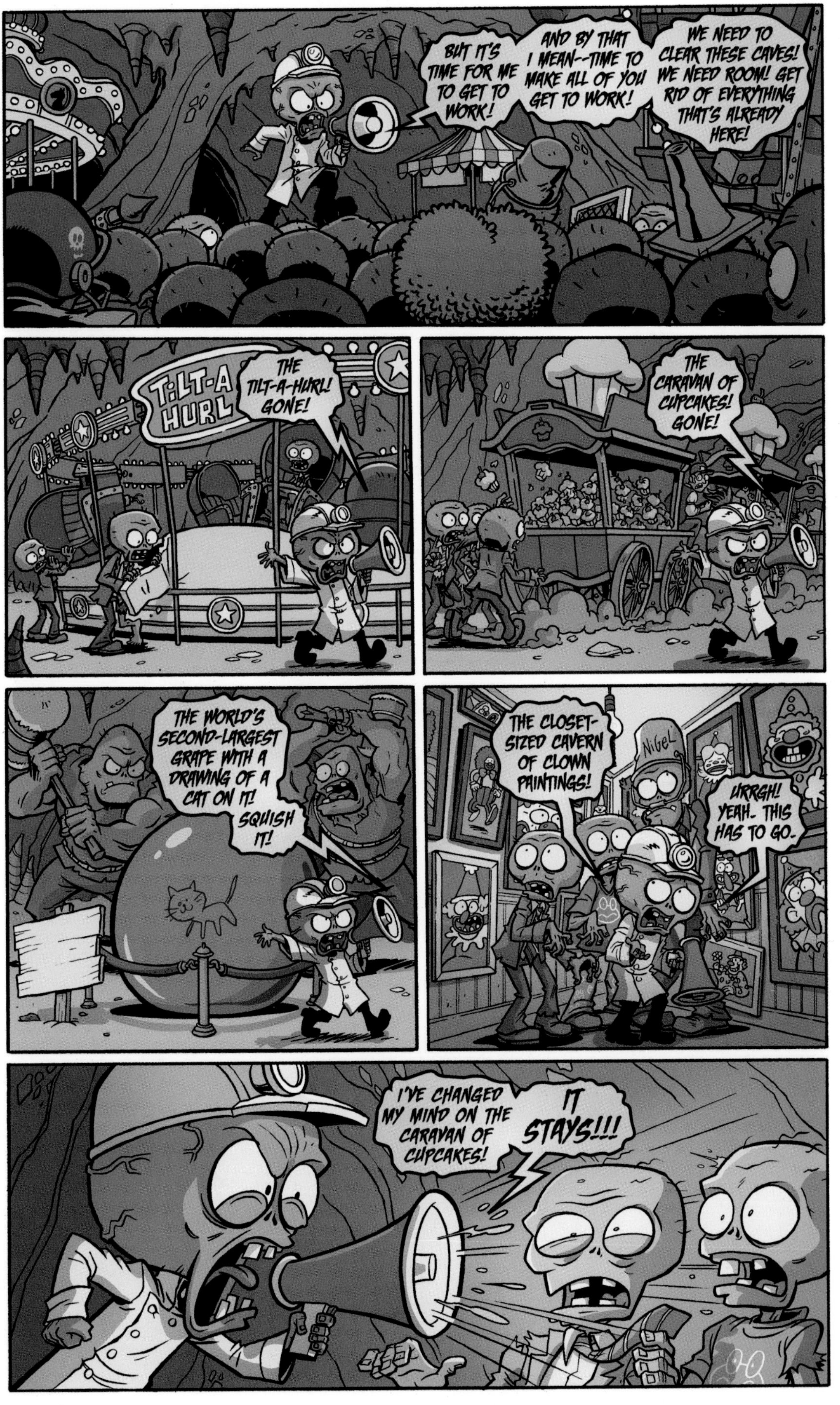
BUT IT'S TIME FOR ME TO GET TO WORK!
AND BY THAT I MEAN--TIME TO MAKE ALL OF YOU GET TO WORK!
WE NEED TO CLEAR THESE CAVES! WE NEED ROOM! GET RID OF EVERYTHING THAT'S ALREADY HERE!
TILT-A HURL
THE TILT-A-HURL! GONE!
THE CARAVAN OF CUPCAKES! GONE!
THE WORLD'S SECOND-LARGEST GRAPE WITH A DRAWING OF A CAT ON IT!
SQUISH IT!
THE CLOSET-SIZED CAVERN OF CLOWN PAINTINGS!
NIGEL
URRGH! YEAH. THIS HAS TO GO.
I'VE CHANGED MY MIND ON THE CARAVAN OF CUPCAKES!
IT STAYS!!!

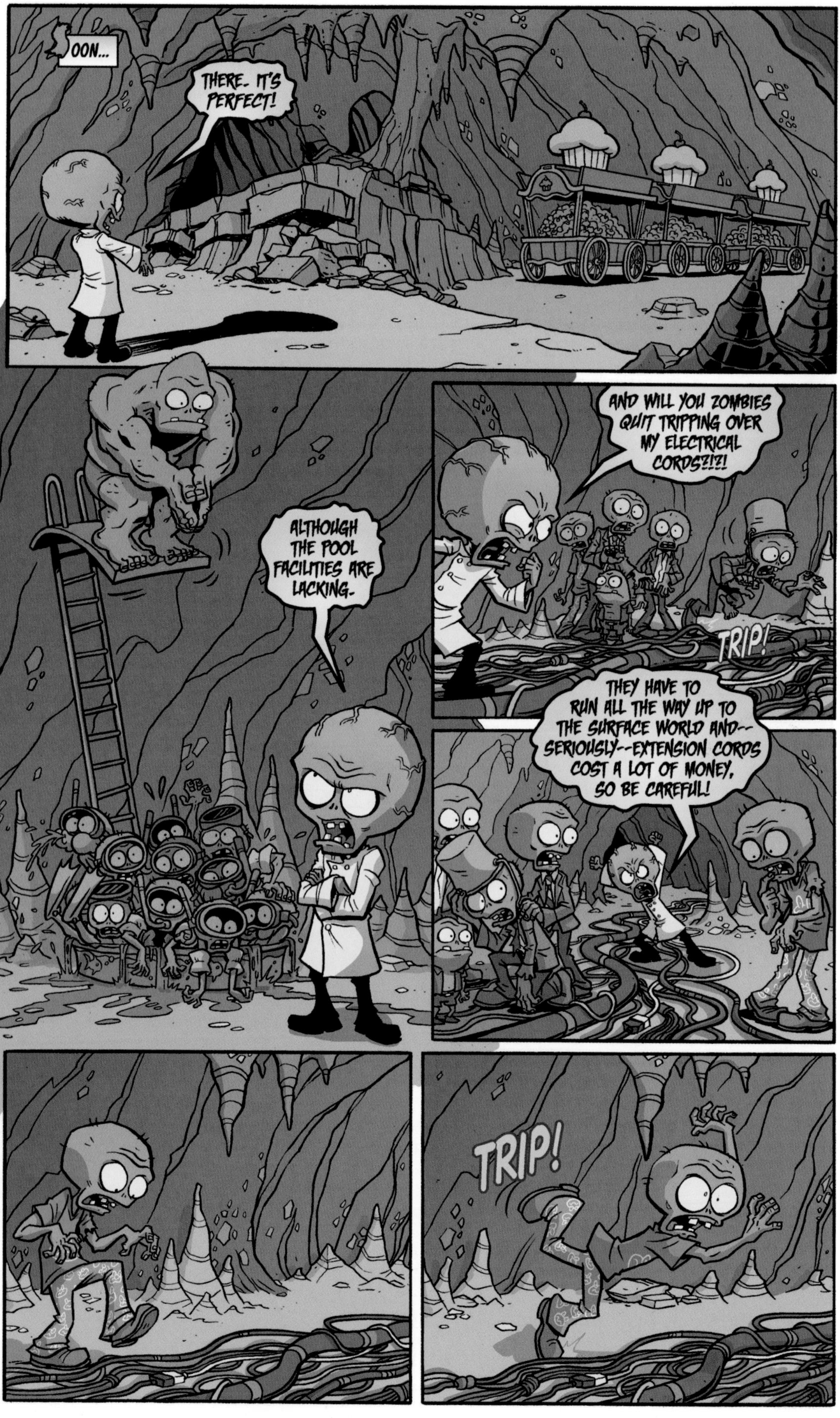
SOON...
THERE. IT'S PERFECT!
ALTHOUGH THE POOL FACILITIES ARE LACKING.
AND WILL YOU ZOMBIES QUIT TRIPPING OVER MY ELECTRICAL CORDS?!?!
TRIP!
THEY HAVE TO RUN ALL THE WAY UP TO THE SURFACE WORLD AND--SERIOUSLY--EXTENSION CORDS COST A LOT OF MONEY, SO BE CAREFUL!
TRIP!

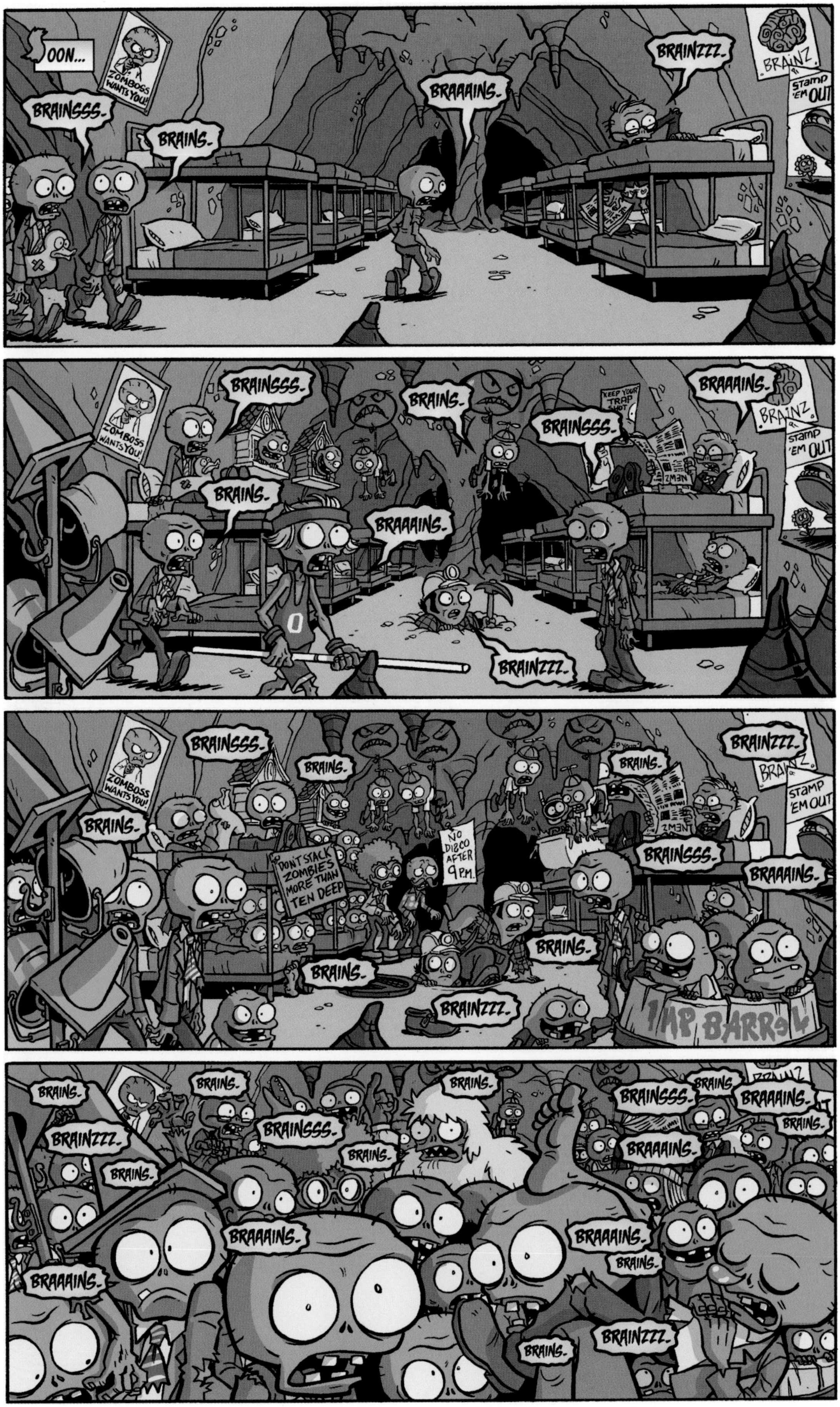
SOON...
ZOMBOSS WANTS YOU!
BRAINSSS.
BRAINS.
BRAAAINS.
BRAINZZZ.
BRAINZ
STAMP 'EM OUT
ZOMBOSS WANTS YOU!
BRAINSSS.
BRAINS.
KEEP YOUR TRAP SHUT
BRAINSSS.
BRAAAINS.
BRAINZ
STAMP 'EM OUT
BRAINS.
BRAAAINS.
BRAINZZZ.
ZOMBOSS WANTS YOU!
BRAINSSS.
BRAINS.
BRAINS.
BRAINZZZ.
STAMP 'EM OUT
BRAINS.
DON'T STACK ZOMBIES MORE THAN TEN DEEP
NO DISCO AFTER 9 P.M.
BRAINSSS.
BRAAAINS.
BRAINS.
BRAINS.
BRAINZZZ.
IMP BARREL
BRAINS.
BRAINS.
BRAINS.
BRAINSSS.
BRAINS
BRAAAINS.
BRAINZZZ.
BRAINSSS.
BRAINS.
BRAINS.
BRAAAINS.
BRAINS.
BRAAAINS.
BRAAAINS.
BRAINS.
BRAAAINS.
BRAINS.
BRAINZZZ.

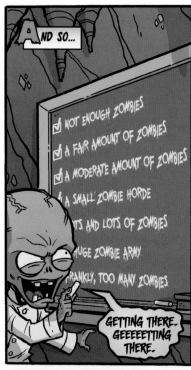

AND SO...

☑ NOT ENOUGH ZOMBIES
☑ A FAIR AMOUNT OF ZOMBIES
☑ A MODERATE AMOUNT OF ZOMBIES
☑ A SMALL ZOMBIE HORDE
...TS AND LOTS OF ZOMBIES
... HUGE ZOMBIE ARMY
... FRANKLY, TOO MANY ZOMBIES

GETTING THERE. GEEEEETTING THERE.

YES...THIS UNDERGROUND COMPLEX OF CAVES IS A PERFECT FACILITY.

HERE, NOTHING CAN GO WRONG. HERE, THERE IS NOTHING TO DISTURB ME.

I MAY AS WELL REST FOR A MOMENT AND ENJOY SOME DELICIOUS POP SMARTS, THE BRAIN-FLAVORED TREAT!

ZZZ ZZZ ZATCH!!

FROOOOGPANTS.

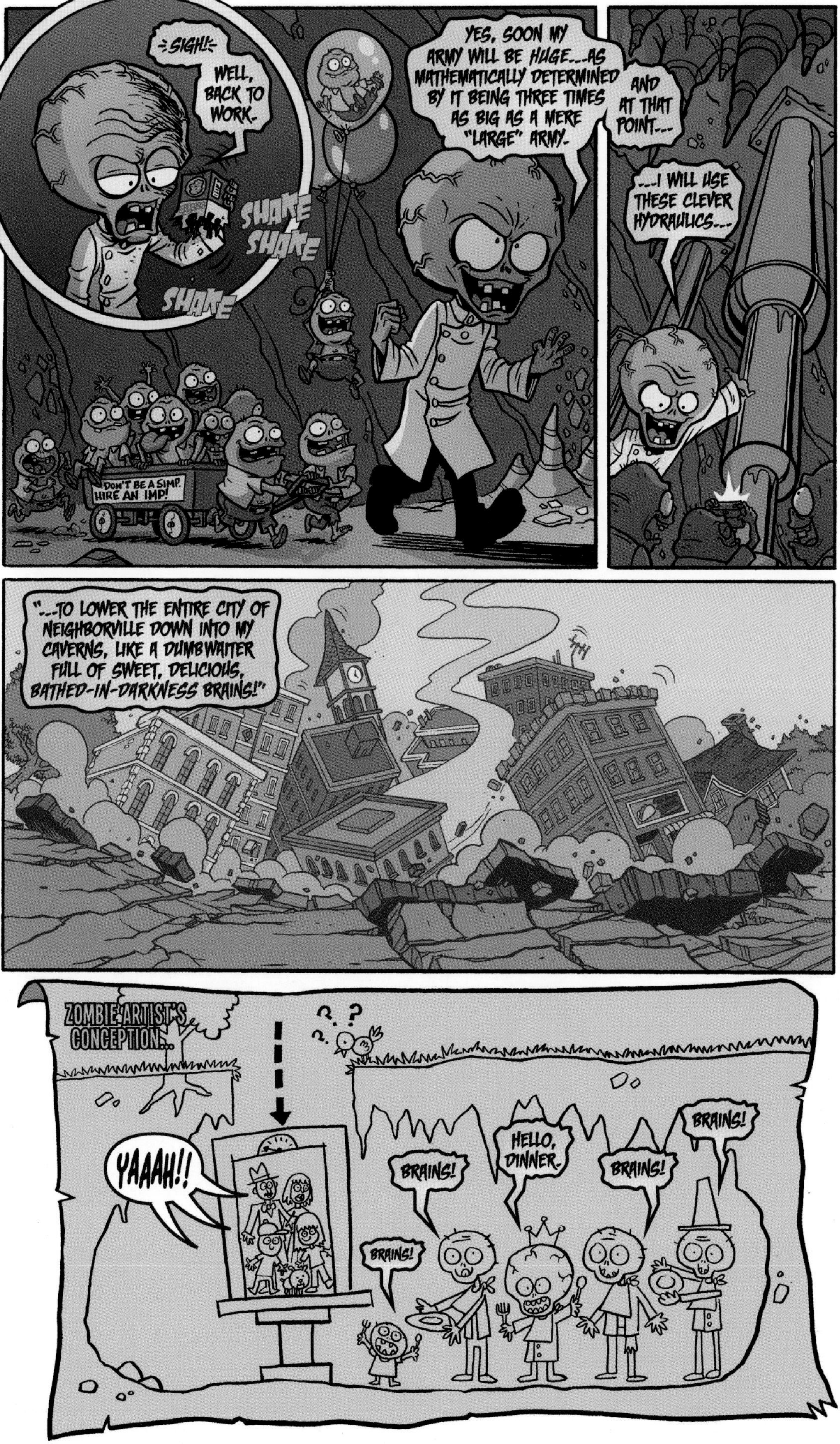
SIGH!
WELL, BACK TO WORK.
SHAKE
SHAKE
SHAKE
YES, SOON MY ARMY WILL BE HUGE...AS MATHEMATICALLY DETERMINED BY IT BEING THREE TIMES AS BIG AS A MERE "LARGE" ARMY.
DON'T BE A SIMP. HIRE AN IMP!
AND AT THAT POINT...
...I WILL USE THESE CLEVER HYDRAULICS...
"...TO LOWER THE ENTIRE CITY OF NEIGHBORVILLE DOWN INTO MY CAVERNS, LIKE A DUMBWAITER FULL OF SWEET, DELICIOUS, BATHED-IN-DARKNESS BRAINS!"
ZOMBIE ARTIST'S CONCEPTION...
YAAAH!!
BRAINS!
BRAINS!
HELLO, DINNER.
BRAINS!
BRAINS!

MEANWHILE...

NATE? DO YOU KNOW WHERE MY UNCLE DAVE IS?

CRAZY DAVE? YOU MEAN WHERE HE IS? HOW WOULD I KNOW WHERE HE IS?

I MEAN, IT'S NOT LIKE HE AND I HAVE BEEN WORKING IN SECRET ANYWHERE! DOING SOMETHING, LIKE, YOU KNOW...

...TRYING TO MAKE MOOD ICE CREAM, ICE CREAM THAT CHANGES ACCORDING TO MOODS, LIKE A MOOD RING.

HA HA HA! THAT WOULD BE SO SILLY! WHO EVEN BROUGHT THAT UP?

NATE. IS THAT WHAT YOU AND UNCLE DAVE ARE DOING?

YES, THAT'S EXACTLY WHAT WE'RE DOING.

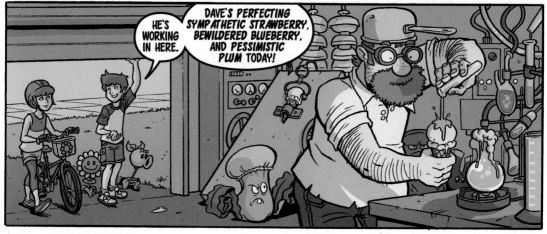

HE'S WORKING IN HERE.

DAVE'S PERFECTING SYMPATHETIC STRAWBERRY, BEWILDERED BLUEBERRY, AND PESSIMISTIC PLUM TODAY!

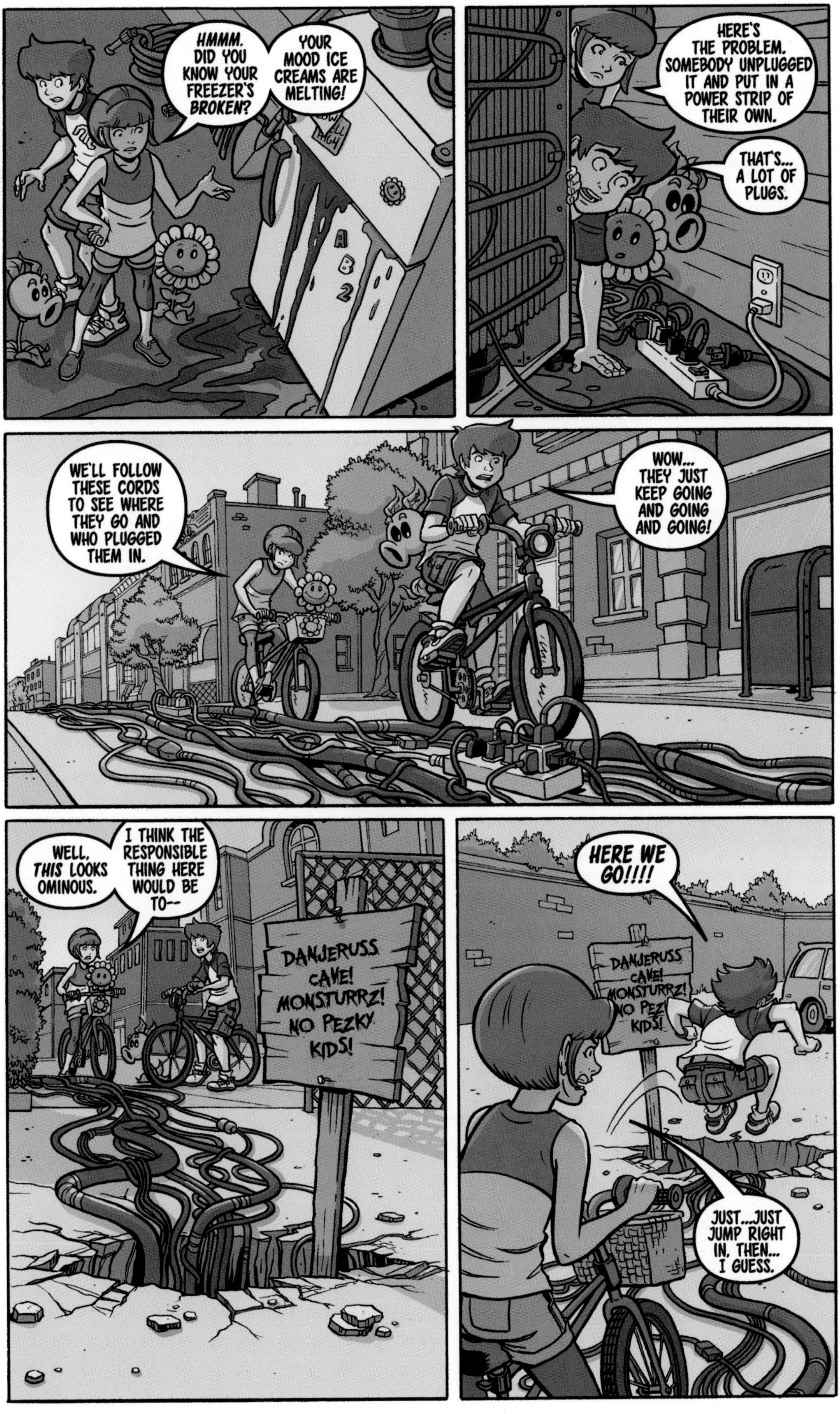
HMMM. DID YOU KNOW YOUR FREEZER'S BROKEN?
YOUR MOOD ICE CREAMS ARE MELTING!
HERE'S THE PROBLEM. SOMEBODY UNPLUGGED IT AND PUT IN A POWER STRIP OF THEIR OWN.
THAT'S... A LOT OF PLUGS.
WE'LL FOLLOW THESE CORDS TO SEE WHERE THEY GO AND WHO PLUGGED THEM IN.
WOW... THEY JUST KEEP GOING AND GOING AND GOING!
WELL, *THIS* LOOKS OMINOUS.
I THINK THE RESPONSIBLE THING HERE WOULD BE TO--
DANJERUSS CAVE! MONSTURRZ! NO PEZKY KIDS!
HERE WE GO!!!!
DANJERUSS CAVE! MONSTURRZ! NO PEZ KIDS!
JUST...JUST JUMP RIGHT IN, THEN... I GUESS.

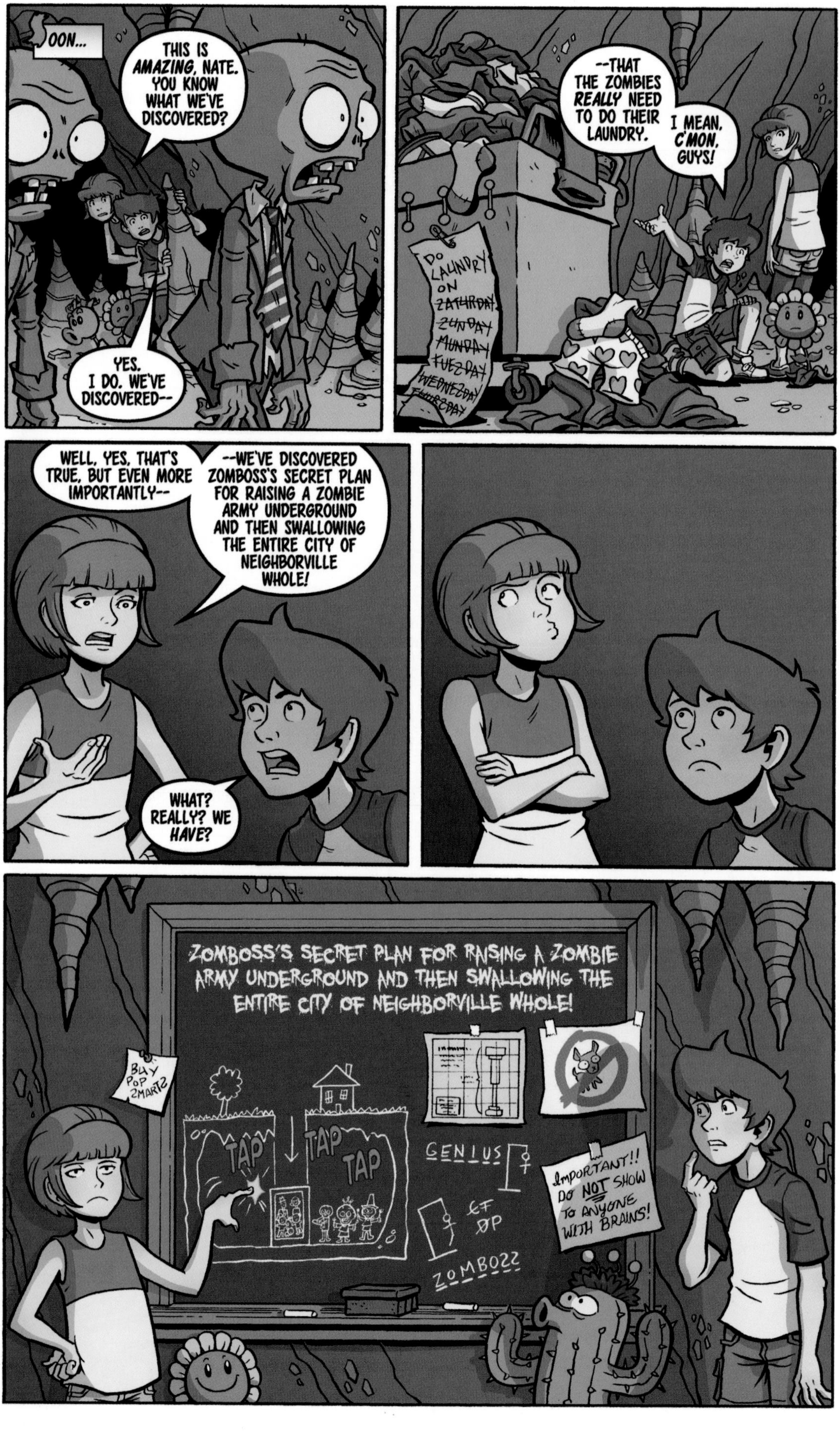
SOON...
THIS IS AMAZING, NATE. YOU KNOW WHAT WE'VE DISCOVERED?
YES. I DO. WE'VE DISCOVERED--
--THAT THE ZOMBIES REALLY NEED TO DO THEIR LAUNDRY.
I MEAN, C'MON, GUYS!
DO LAUNDRY ON
ZATURDAY
ZUNDAY
MUNDAY
TUEZDAY
WEDNEZDAY
THURZDAY
WELL, YES, THAT'S TRUE, BUT EVEN MORE IMPORTANTLY--
--WE'VE DISCOVERED ZOMBOSS'S SECRET PLAN FOR RAISING A ZOMBIE ARMY UNDERGROUND AND THEN SWALLOWING THE ENTIRE CITY OF NEIGHBORVILLE WHOLE!
WHAT? REALLY? WE HAVE?
ZOMBOSS'S SECRET PLAN FOR RAISING A ZOMBIE ARMY UNDERGROUND AND THEN SWALLOWING THE ENTIRE CITY OF NEIGHBORVILLE WHOLE!
BUY POP ZMARTZ
TAP
TAP
TAP
GENIUS
IMPORTANT!! DO NOT SHOW TO ANYONE WITH BRAINS!
ZOMBOZZ

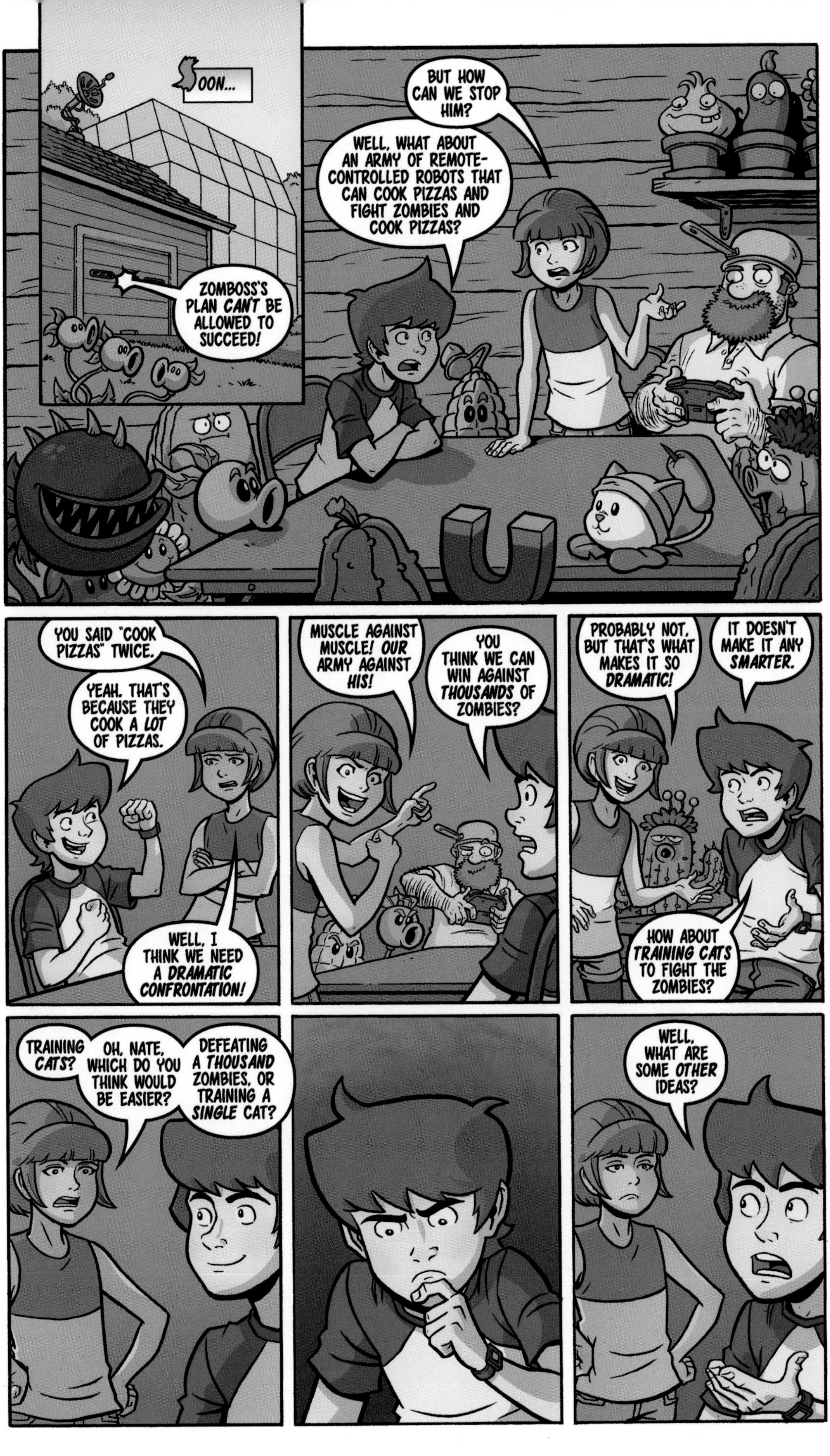
SOON...
ZOMBOSS'S PLAN CAN'T BE ALLOWED TO SUCCEED!
BUT HOW CAN WE STOP HIM?
WELL, WHAT ABOUT AN ARMY OF REMOTE-CONTROLLED ROBOTS THAT CAN COOK PIZZAS AND FIGHT ZOMBIES AND COOK PIZZAS?
YOU SAID "COOK PIZZAS" TWICE.
YEAH. THAT'S BECAUSE THEY COOK A LOT OF PIZZAS.
WELL, I THINK WE NEED A DRAMATIC CONFRONTATION!
MUSCLE AGAINST MUSCLE! OUR ARMY AGAINST HIS!
YOU THINK WE CAN WIN AGAINST THOUSANDS OF ZOMBIES?
PROBABLY NOT, BUT THAT'S WHAT MAKES IT SO DRAMATIC!
IT DOESN'T MAKE IT ANY SMARTER.
HOW ABOUT TRAINING CATS TO FIGHT THE ZOMBIES?
TRAINING CATS?
OH, NATE, WHICH DO YOU THINK WOULD BE EASIER?
DEFEATING A THOUSAND ZOMBIES, OR TRAINING A SINGLE CAT?
WELL, WHAT ARE SOME OTHER IDEAS?

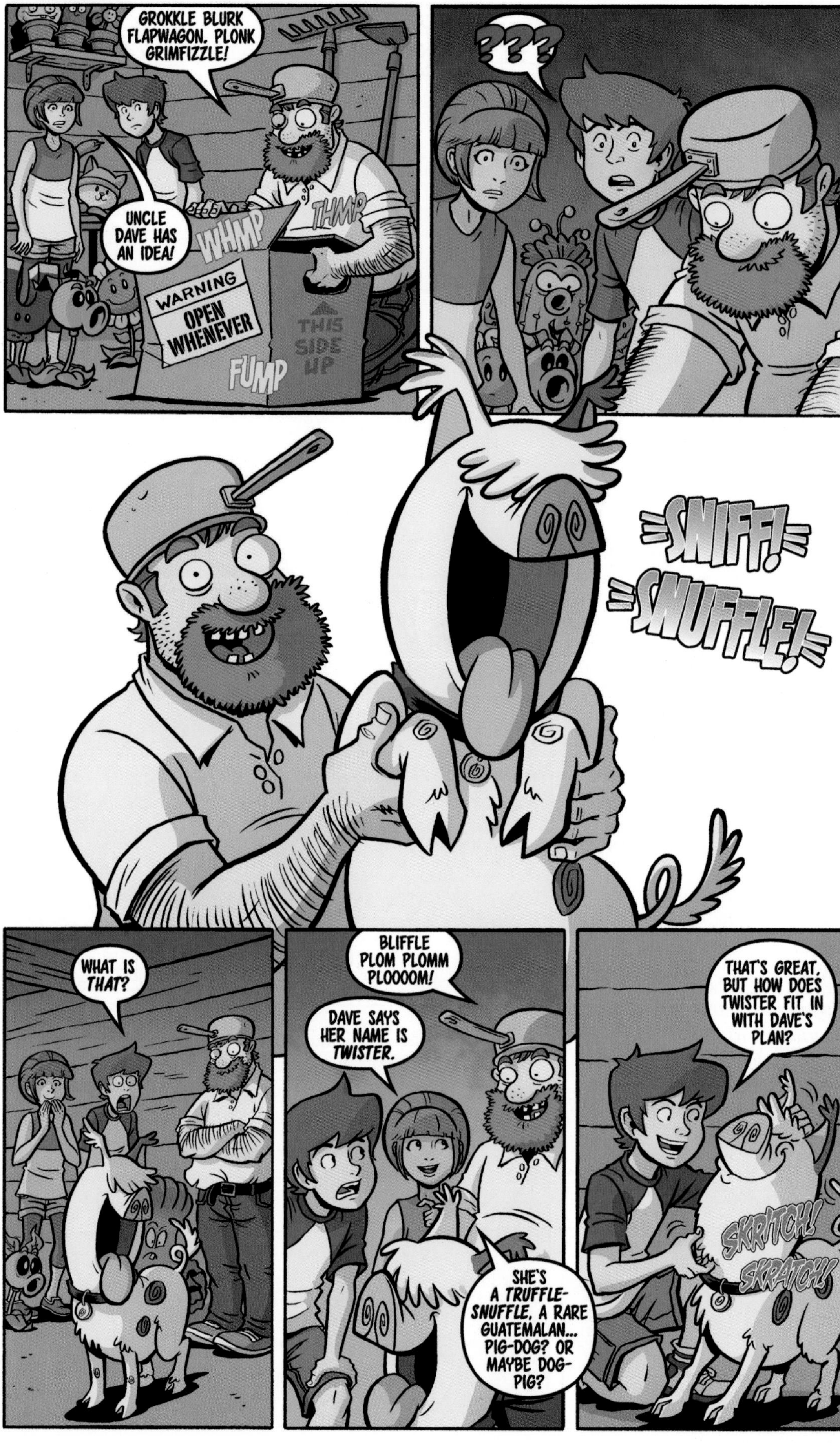
GROKKLE BLURK FLAPWAGON. PLONK GRIMFIZZLE!
UNCLE DAVE HAS AN IDEA!
THMP
WHMP
WARNING
OPEN WHENEVER
THIS SIDE UP
FUMP
???
SNIFF!
SNUFFLE!
WHAT IS THAT?
BLIFFLE PLOM PLOMM PLOOOOM!
DAVE SAYS HER NAME IS TWISTER.
SHE'S A TRUFFLE-SNUFFLE, A RARE GUATEMALAN... PIG-DOG? OR MAYBE DOG-PIG?
THAT'S GREAT, BUT HOW DOES TWISTER FIT IN WITH DAVE'S PLAN?
SKRITCH!
SKRATCH!

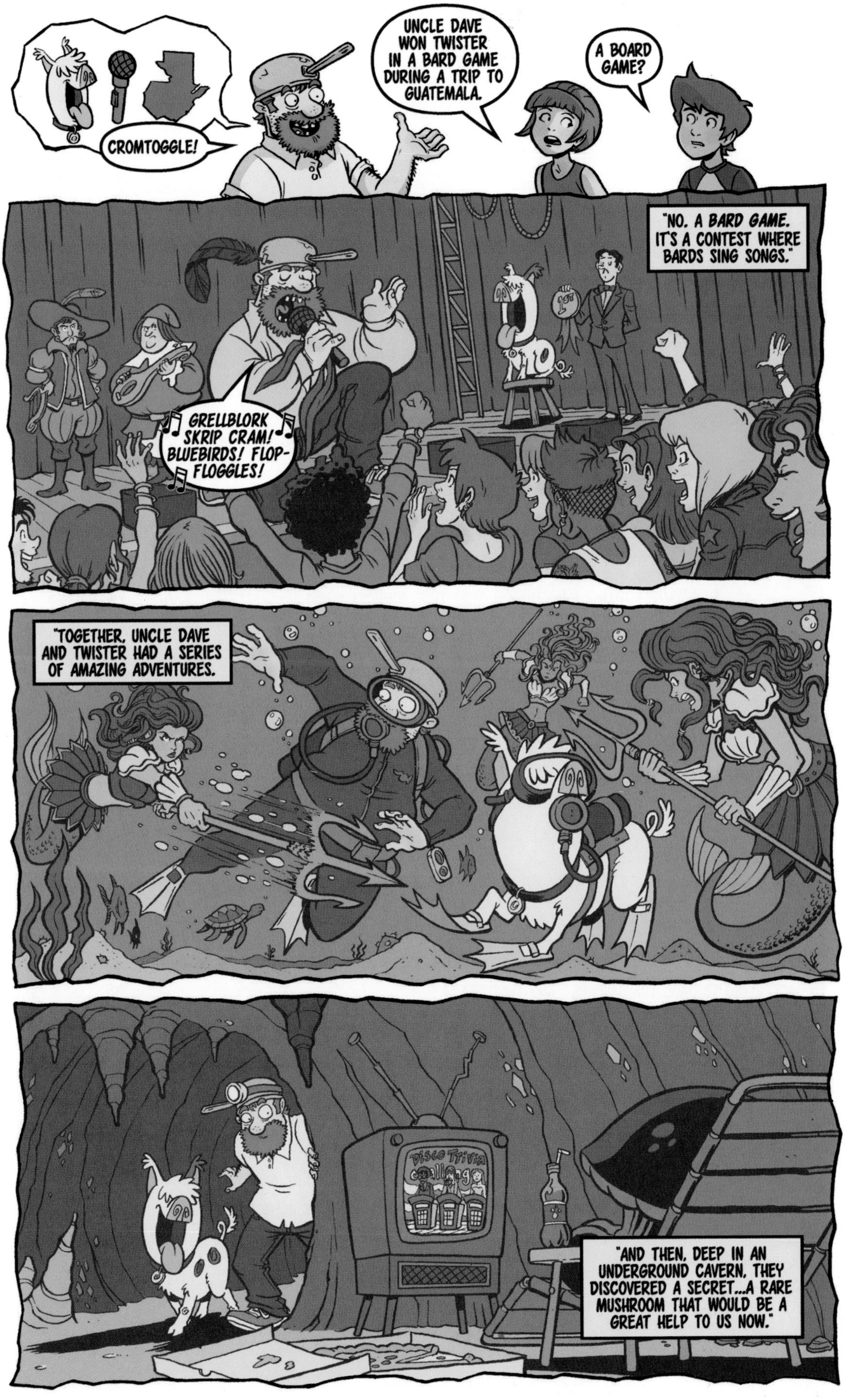
CROMTOGGLE!
UNCLE DAVE WON TWISTER IN A BARD GAME DURING A TRIP TO GUATEMALA.
A BOARD GAME?
"NO. A *BARD GAME*. IT'S A CONTEST WHERE BARDS SING SONGS."
GRELLBLORK SKRIP CRAM! BLUEBIRDS! FLOP-FLOGGLES!
"TOGETHER, UNCLE DAVE AND TWISTER HAD A SERIES OF AMAZING ADVENTURES.
"AND THEN, DEEP IN AN UNDERGROUND CAVERN, THEY DISCOVERED A SECRET...A RARE MUSHROOM THAT WOULD BE A GREAT HELP TO US NOW."

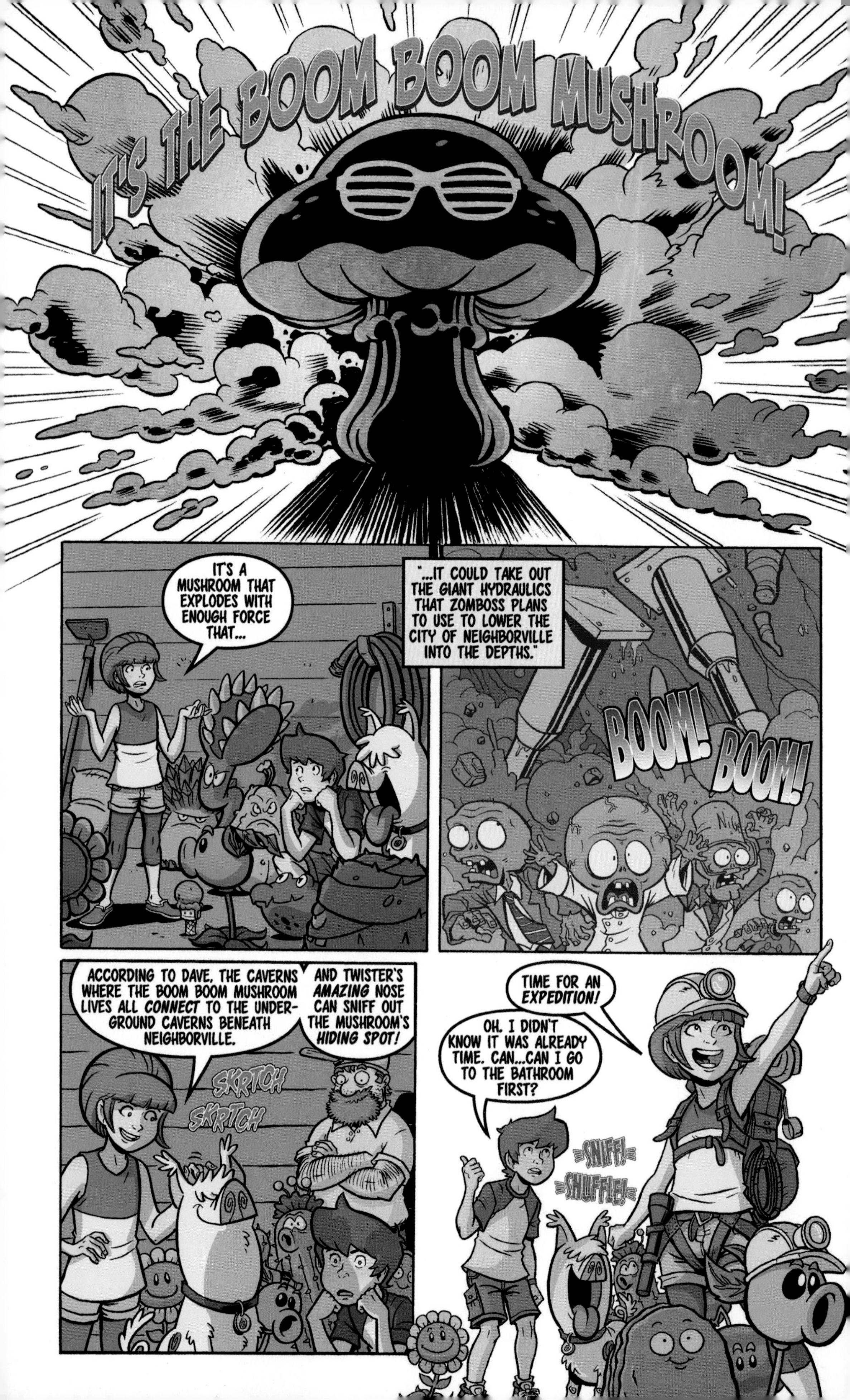
IT'S THE BOOM BOOM MUSHROOM!
IT'S A MUSHROOM THAT EXPLODES WITH ENOUGH FORCE THAT...
"...IT COULD TAKE OUT THE GIANT HYDRAULICS THAT ZOMBOSS PLANS TO USE TO LOWER THE CITY OF NEIGHBORVILLE INTO THE DEPTHS."
BOOM! BOOM!
ACCORDING TO DAVE, THE CAVERNS WHERE THE BOOM BOOM MUSHROOM LIVES ALL CONNECT TO THE UNDER-GROUND CAVERNS BENEATH NEIGHBORVILLE.
AND TWISTER'S AMAZING NOSE CAN SNIFF OUT THE MUSHROOM'S HIDING SPOT!
SKRTCH
SKRTCH
TIME FOR AN EXPEDITION!
OH, I DIDN'T KNOW IT WAS ALREADY TIME. CAN...CAN I GO TO THE BATHROOM FIRST?
SNIFF!
SNUFFLE!

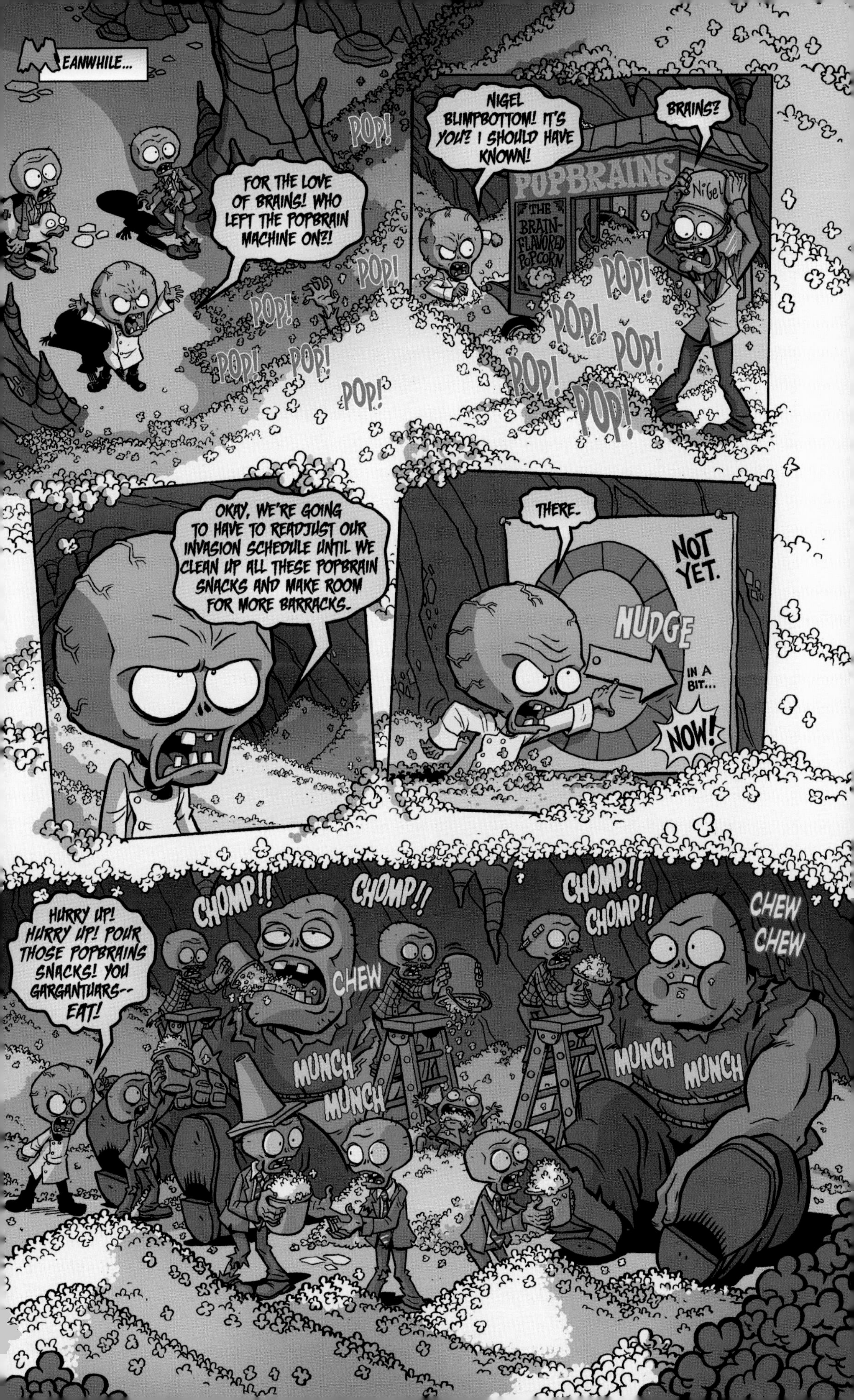
MEANWHILE...
FOR THE LOVE OF BRAINS! WHO LEFT THE POPBRAIN MACHINE ON?!
POP!
POP!
POP!
POP!
POP!
POP!
NIGEL BLIMPBOTTOM! IT'S YOU? I SHOULD HAVE KNOWN!
BRAINS?
POPBRAINS
THE BRAIN-FLAVORED POPCORN
NiGel
POP!
POP!
POP!
POP!
POP!
OKAY, WE'RE GOING TO HAVE TO READJUST OUR INVASION SCHEDULE UNTIL WE CLEAN UP ALL THESE POPBRAIN SNACKS AND MAKE ROOM FOR MORE BARRACKS.
THERE.
NOT YET.
NUDGE
IN A BIT...
NOW!
HURRY UP! HURRY UP! POUR THOSE POPBRAINS SNACKS! YOU GARGANTUARS--EAT!
CHOMP!!
CHOMP!!
CHOMP!!
CHOMP!!
CHEW
CHEW
CHEW
MUNCH
MUNCH
MUNCH
MUNCH

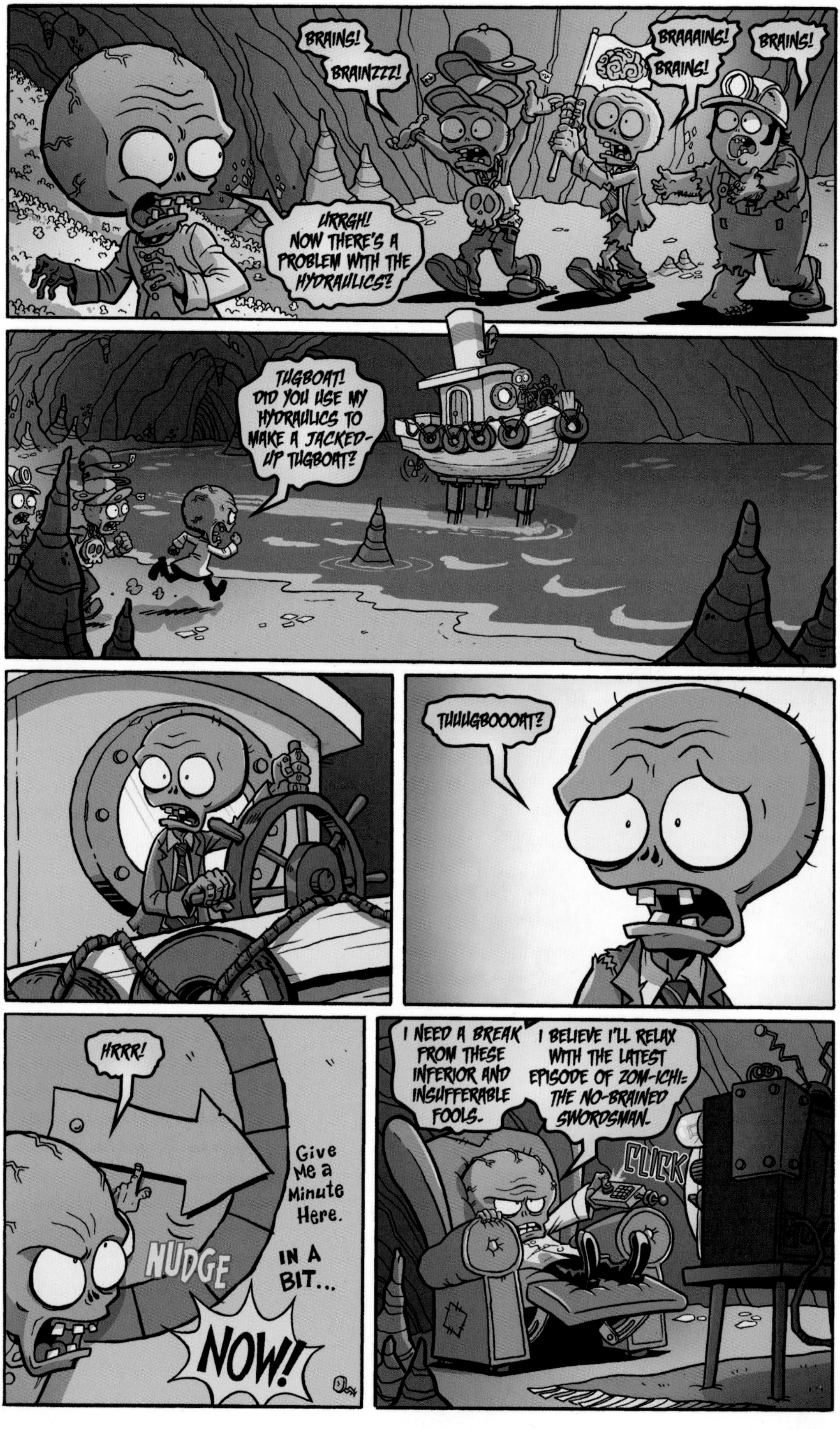

BRAINS!
BRAINZZZ!
BRAAAINS!
BRAINS!
BRAINS!
URRGH! NOW THERE'S A PROBLEM WITH THE HYDRAULICS?
TUGBOAT! DID YOU USE MY HYDRAULICS TO MAKE A JACKED-UP TUGBOAT?
TUUUGBOOOAT?
HRRR!
NUDGE
Give Me a Minute Here.
IN A BIT...
NOW!!
I NEED A BREAK FROM THESE INFERIOR AND INSUFFERABLE FOOLS.
I BELIEVE I'LL RELAX WITH THE LATEST EPISODE OF ZOM-ICHI: THE NO-BRAINED SWORDSMAN.
CLICK

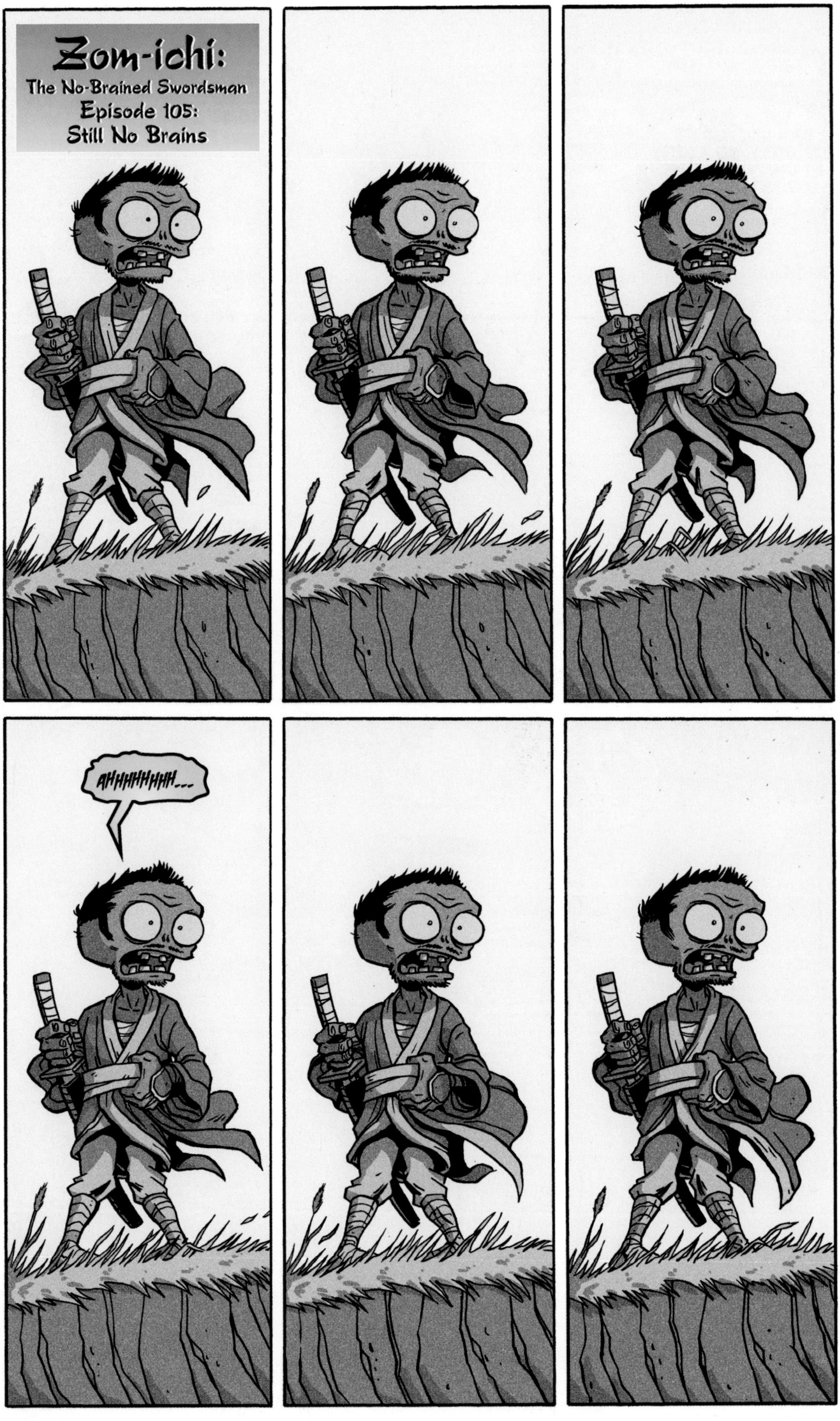
Zom-ichi:
The No-Brained Swordsman
Episode 105:
Still No Brains
AHHHHHHHH...

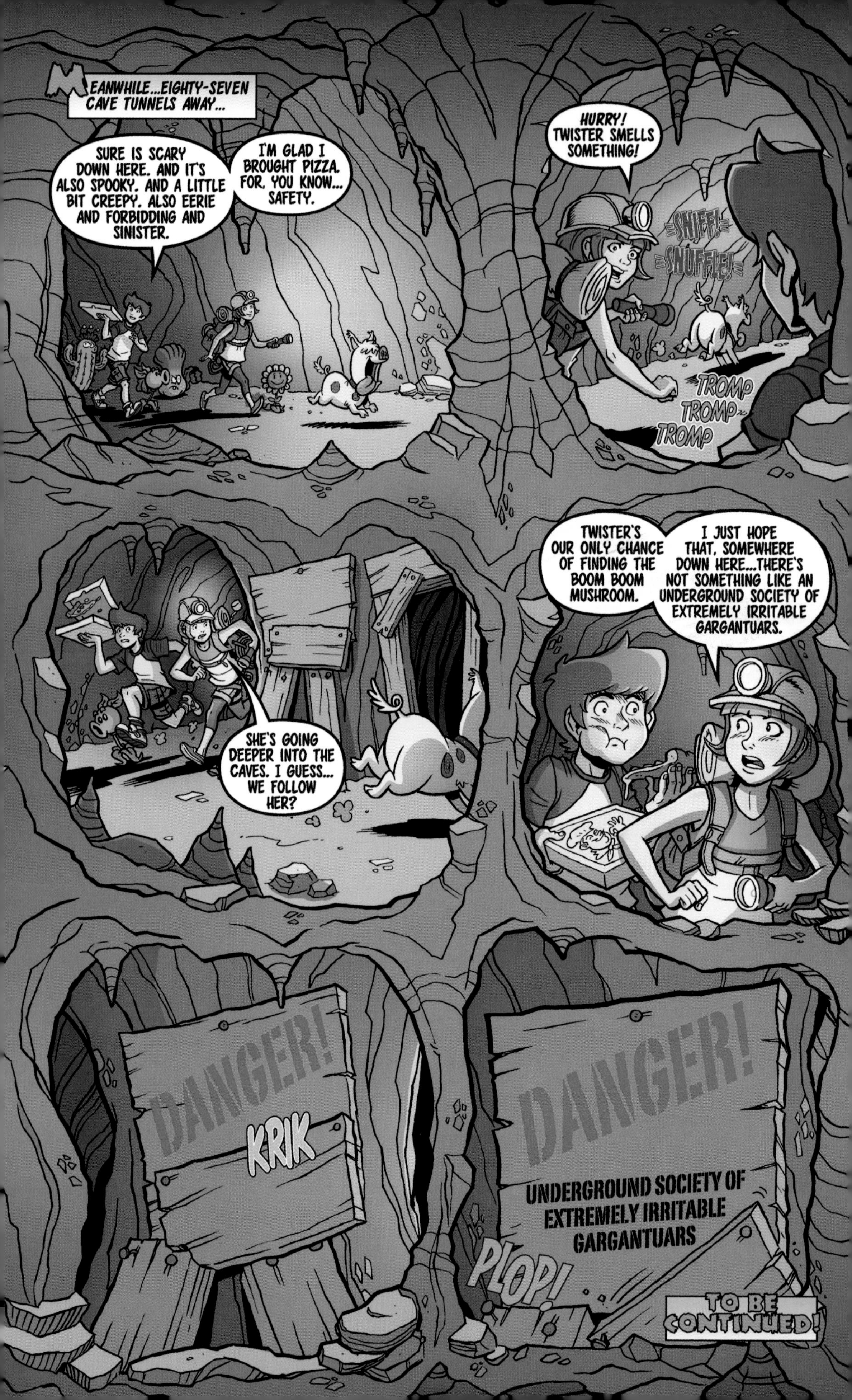
MEANWHILE...EIGHTY-SEVEN CAVE TUNNELS AWAY...
SURE IS SCARY DOWN HERE. AND IT'S ALSO SPOOKY. AND A LITTLE BIT CREEPY. ALSO EERIE AND FORBIDDING AND SINISTER.
I'M GLAD I BROUGHT PIZZA. FOR, YOU KNOW... SAFETY.
HURRY! TWISTER SMELLS SOMETHING!
SNIFF!
SNUFFLE!
TROMP
TROMP
TROMP
SHE'S GOING DEEPER INTO THE CAVES. I GUESS... WE FOLLOW HER?
TWISTER'S OUR ONLY CHANCE OF FINDING THE BOOM BOOM MUSHROOM.
I JUST HOPE THAT, SOMEWHERE DOWN HERE...THERE'S NOT SOMETHING LIKE AN UNDERGROUND SOCIETY OF EXTREMELY IRRITABLE GARGANTUARS.
DANGER!
KRIK
DANGER!
UNDERGROUND SOCIETY OF EXTREMELY IRRITABLE GARGANTUARS
PLOP!
TO BE CONTINUED!